I0536993

# STORY TELLING FORTY TWO

# Strands

## A Book of Poems by

## Richard Seal

# *Strands*

Published by

Percychatteybooks Publishing

ISBN 978 1 9162712 7 2

## STORY TELLING FORTY TWO

# *Strands*

I have always felt that there is something particularly magical about writing poetry. Just an idea or a word or two is usually enough to get started - the poem appears in the silence, the space between thought and feeling.

Richard Seal
21 June 2020

**para Sandra - el amor siempre**

# Chapter One

Avid star gazer
has no way to comprehend
space beyond Great Bear.

Man did not expect
to die doing DIY.
An insect inspects.

# Weeds

Loves to haul weeds out of the earth,
thick ones with strong roots are the worst.
Although it breaks her back, she knows
a knife works better than a hoe.
Stands up when a patch has been cleared,
relieved green clumps have disappeared.
Has no idea, as she walks away
that insects will now have their say.

Ants, beetles, worms have a pow wow
to share thoughts and ideas on how
normality will be restored.
They know that they can ill afford
to let the human think she's won
and enjoy her day in the sun.
Seething ants gather and bristle,
they will manufacture thistles;
the beetles know they can succeed
in creating lots of bindweed;
making dandelions will be tough
if the worms don't try hard enough.

Creatures meet when work has been done,
ruining the lawn has been such fun.
Each one retreats to take its place
to view the look on woman's face.

# Max

The first thing that she had to know
before she would agree to go
on holiday to anywhere
was 'Will they allow my dog there?'

Could not relax and take the sun
without Max, it would not be fun
seeing sights, with him left at home
to pine in the kennels alone.

In the end she found a chalet
where her best friend could also stay.
Max stayed warm inside, took his ease;
glad not to be strapped into skis.

# Style

In the pretty plaza Jane waits
and watches people celebrate
their own individual styles;
teenagers breeze past with a smile,
cool women brisk on shopping spree,
an old couple's quiet dignity.
Observer gets self-conscious now,
feels a bit scruffy, makes a vow
that she will start to make a mark
in pencil skirt and silken scarves.

# Past Caring

Mother thrashes in her room, gripped
by terminal cancer; this trip
is the final one she will take.
Her children don't know what to make
of a personality washed
overboard. The woman is lost
at sea - pillows flung, sheets torn
and panic stations are the norm.
Stricken, nothing left worth sharing,
goes down with the ship past caring.

# Table

For decades the dining table
took pride of place, strong and stable;
it served the family, earned its space
Had no desire to be replaced,
but in the end time took a toll:
two legs wobbled as it got old.
However, table earned good luck,
deservedly a deal was struck;
to this day it is holding on
while other furniture has gone.
Stands in the shed, never ignored,
proudly holding hammers and saws.

# Chocolate

For Annie nothing can compare
to chocolate; friends would never dare
for birthdays or Christmas to buy
something else for the girl. One tried

giving beauty products one year;
the teenager's smile disappeared
and she applied the evil eye
which made her friend cower and cry.

While Annie has long since grown up
friends know she still can't get enough;
the woman prefers to get lost
deep within a dark chocolate box.

# Unfriend

Social media became her world;
profiles and photos thrilled the girl.
She focused on friends' life events,
details of when they came and went.
Hid her own details all the time,
but following others felt fine.
Shocked when complacency ended -
the teen found herself unfriended.

# Detector

His metal detector takes pride
of place in his life, folks are wide
of the mark when they call him weird.
He knows one day he will appear

triumphantly before them all
holding aloft a wondrous haul
of gold and silver trinkets found
after centuries spent underground.

That moment will be so sublime,
but until then he bides his time;
goes out each day in wind and rain,
unearths washers, bicycle chains.

# Prawns

At the picnic, eyes are half closed
around little smile as she gets lost
in a pot of king prawns, luxuriating
over the distinctive taste and texture
against her tongue. Having blushed
fleetingly at boyfriend's mock shock,
girl enjoys lingering over licking lips;
sticks out her tongue, then giggles.

# Cup Final

On this F.A. Cup Final Day
thousands of fans thronged Wembley Way.
But one team is not having fun,
game seems lost before it's begun:
City's attack is far too weak,
star striker has a hamstring tweak.
Super sub is left in the bench
with gritted teeth and both fists clenched;
at the death feels devastated
as Town's goal is celebrated.


# Technology

Why friends embrace technology
remains a complete mystery
to a girl who prefers to cook
and lose herself in a good book.

She has no interest in staring
down at a screen, never caring
about selfies, pictures of food
which usually serve to intrude

of her feelings of inner calm.
When Wi-Fi is down, not alarmed;
although when YouTube is no go
she misses kitten videos.

# Setback

Facing any setback, Christine
was not a person to be seen
moping or bemoaning her lot;
the woman seized each chance she got

to learn from errors, try again.
Never phased by the heavy rain
she would dance in a storm instead
of opting to remain in bed.

Kept moving forwards when she passed,
Chris kept her best until the last:
her organs helped others to live,
the best donation she could give.

# New Broom

When the old manager retired
next up was a young high flyer.
Lynne was keen to be a new broom
sweeping briskly across the room;
she had a wealth of fresh ideas
which caused resentment and some fear.
At first the woman seemed too tough,
but she lightened up soon enough;
once the boss slackened off the pace,
the dust settled back into place.

# Pens Down

When dreaded moment comes to turn
the paper over, stomach churns
and the final exam can start.
Eventually thundering heart
calms down then adrenaline grips
awhile before composure slips
to a bitten lip and deep frown
when instructed to put pens down.

# Tissue

The lady frowned, took great issue
at sneezing without a tissue;
her grandchildren were always told
she did not want to catch their cold.

Coughing without a shielding hand
she simply could not understand;
the selfishness of such an act
could have a really dire impact.

With hygiene she knew what to do,
went through her life avoiding flu;
but had no chance to make a fuss
when run down by a minibus.

# Marked

The teacher is slumped in her chair,
fighting fatigue, barely aware
the ashtray is full, coffee gone cold.
She loves her job, but feels so old
each time there is an inspection,
withers during observations.
Prepares for hours, but never sure
why books end up strewn on the floor.
Cannot focus, feels slightly sick,
as work is marked with random ticks.

# Front Page

Watching horror headlines each day
made the man want to turn away
from internet and TV news
which made him feel depressed, confused,
filled with fears without form or shape,
with no light relief or escape ...
He changed the channel several times
but ended up with unsolved crimes,
reality, quizzes or soaps.
Just as he felt he could not cope
he found some puppies and kittens
which calmed the soul, man was smitten.
'Animals saved' is the story,
rescuers covered in glory.

# Gate

Melanie came under attack
for being a hypochondriac;
had every symptom known to man,
the doubters could not understand

that she was sick, but took great care
to check the facts, become aware
of dangers lurking in the germs.
Eventually she came to terms

with the fact she would end her days
before her friends; yet somehow stayed
alive the longest. Woman's fate
was to be the creakiest gate.


# Best Man

As Best Man stood watching the bride
beaming in the carriage beside
her husband, he ruefully smiled
to himself. For a little while
they had dated, Colleen had been
a major crush throughout his teens.
However, the girl in the end
quite clearly preferred his best friend.
In his mind he replayed his toast
to the couple he loved the most.

Beneath the pine tree
caterpillar takes the shape
of a harmless twig.

Words thought not spoken
metastasise, burrow deep,
somehow find a voice.

Bolt of forked lightning
lets rip on the mountainside.
Primordial strike.

Can sense in her eyes
other dimension concealed.
Smile reveals nothing.

Right from the start, girl
felt different from others; sat
stony faced in games.

# Slow Motion

Smiles watching herself lost in play
as a child on her tenth birthday.
Parents' special treat was inspired:
a video camera was hired.
Sees girl blowing out her candles,
then showing off plastic bangles.
Replaying that day, feels so glad
that she threw her arms around dad.
Now overcome with emotion
at joy captured in slow motion.

# Bone of Contention

The couple's bone of contention
was the issue of retention
of the kittens born to Princess.
Their three dogs were less than impressed.

While the little ones were adored
by both of them, could they afford
the vet's bills and the cost of food?
Yet splitting the eight seemed so rude.

Agreement was reached on a plan
to satisfy these feline fans:
keep them for now (Neither believed
that their furry children would leave).

# Sleeper

Ever since the man was a boy
he has not had a lot of joy
in achieving a good night's sleep
despite attempts at counting sheep.

He has tried many different ways
to drop off, struggling through each day;
often exhausted, second hand;
his workmates could not understand

his decision to work from home.
Things improved when he was alone,
felt productive, achieved much more
when working from midnight to four.

# Y2K

He remembers impending arrival
of 2000 threatening survival
of computer systems. An awesome crash
seemed likely to burn all laptops to ash.
Millennium bug fears caused untold grief,
but after wailing and gnashing of teeth
PCs were nonchalant as the year turned;
sneered at humankind, remained unconcerned.

# Honey

Being called 'sweetheart' is a curse
while 'darling' seems a little worse.
One work colleague calls her 'honey'
all the time, which is not funny.
Woman silently boils and seethes
to herself, she truly believes
people do it time and again
just to wind her up, yank her chain.
Yet never wonders if folk hate
her calling them 'love', 'son' or 'mate'.

# Knack

Something else lay beyond the smile
of a girl who lacked spite and guile.
Tried briefly to be serious
but gave up - it seemed such a fuss

to try to act grown up, mature.
What did it mean? She was not sure.
Being solemn, down-beat or grave
seemed a painful way to behave.

In the end refused to hold back
her love for life - girl had a knack
for comedy, loved to be daft
and lifted the room with her laugh.

# Daft

The first time that big sister laughed
at Elizabeth, called her daft
was when her dolly's arm came off -
The older girl said she was soft.

Jackie always appeared so cool,
top dog at home as well as school;
teased by her sister every day,
Liz felt inferior always.

The younger girl bided her time,
planned to commit a heinous crime.
But sadly failed to understand
that not everything goes to plan.

If caught, Liz knew she faced her doom,
yet crept into big sister's room.
With felt pen wrote 'Jackie is dumb'
on a pink skirt borrowed from mum.

# Tablets

Frowning down at row of tablets
lined up for him to take each day,
Bill cannot help feeling regret
that his routine is now this way.
But in an instant checks himself
- so what if his pills leave him cold?
At eighty man still has his health
and privilege of being old.

# Trickster

Could not resist practical jokes,
she played them on the warehouse blokes.
Stuck boxes together with glue
and no one seemed to have a clue

it was her who acted so mean
ringing down for buckets of steam
from the trainee on his first day;
tried his best, but there was no way

he could track down any hot ice.
Next day the trickster was enticed
to HR - morale took a dive
with a bogus P45.

# Ball

Once liked playing football with friends
but the lad found that in the end
games were getting harder, faster,
more competitive, nastier.
Lad hung on in there for a while,
but was told he lacked skill and style.
He found himself kicking a ball
alone against the garden wall.
Tried a comeback but it fell flat -
he lost fourteen nil to his cat.

# Woman Alone

On an all-male team, held her own:
cool and calm, a woman alone.
One of the boys with all the men,
Amanda bantered now and then;
light-hearted flirting was okay,
but did not hesitate to say
when a colleague had crossed the line.
She worked hard and bided her time,
before long became number one.
In charge for a while, then moved on.

# Drink

The woman used to like a drink
a whisky chaser helped her think,
while there was no denying fear
and doubts reduced with a few beers.

She had a reputation too
for partying, knew what to do
to help events go with a swing
after downing Singapore Slings.

On doctor's orders cut right back,
but instantly she felt the lack;
so told herself wine was okay
when there was a 'y' in the day.

## Fridge Magnet

Señorita has been dancing
on a fridge magnet for ten years;
Seeing her has been enhancing
Dan's life ever since she appeared.
Wonders about lady's story,
hopes she still puts on a great show.
For this man, in splendid glory,
she will always dance Flamenco.

## Authority

Susan always had words to say
on every topic, knew the way
that everybody should proceed;
only her advice could succeed.

The lady held forth over tea
and cake, would issue a decree
that failing to listen to her
would make a disaster occur.

The thing that turned things on their head
was losing her favourite cat Ned;
he came back when she passed the test,
now declares that felines know best.

# One

Loves the rapport, forming a bond
when meeting people one-to-one;
she feels relaxed and connected,
fully involved and respected.
However, when two becomes three
the woman feels a bit less free,
while a social event with four
quite quickly turns into a bore.
If there are more people than that,
she will stay at home with her cat.

# Food

From childhood he had thought it rude
to turn down an offer of food;
no matter fried or fricasseed
the youngster thought he had it made.

Yet he had an Achilles heel:
green vegetables blighted a meal.
Lad could not abide cauliflower,
while Brussels sprouts made him cower;

peas would not allow him to thrive,
while spinach brought him out in hives;
Knew vegetables were a mistake,
replaced them all with carrot cake.

# Cocoon

Coming into wake his wife finds
the lady wound tightly inside
a bedsheet and duvet cocoon,
not surfacing anytime soon.
Sitting beside her for a while,
in silence, her face makes him smile;
the peace that he hopes she can keep
arrives without effort in sleep.

# Comedy

Spent a lifetime loving laughter.
Class clown - there was no one dafter,
all his friends and teachers agreed.
Watched comedy films on TV
all the time to get hints and tips.
Wrote material, tried to slip
gags into chat to try them out.

Before long he was in no doubt
that the stand-up comic was King
and he would not let anything
hold him back. Submitted sketches
which would never be accepted,
but each rejection could be seen
being played out in his routines.
Toured to the end, never retired
'It's only the jokes that get tired.'

# Chapter Two

The woodlouse's life
has not been a waste; body
now pulled by an ant.

The thin line between
good and evil blurs by day;
second sight at night.

# Couplets

The teacher tried to be a card,
and make students laugh, tried so hard
to be eccentric every day,
behaving in unusual ways.

Impressions tended to fall flat,
one liners too, so soon stopped that.
Then came up with a great idea
to make his pupils hold him dear:

Put rhyming couplets on worksheets
for each class, did not dare repeat
the same once twice - he had his pride,
but needed to search far and wide

for inspiration. Very soon
the well ran dry; he sensed his doom,
an air of panic seemed so grim
he got a team of writers in.

Expenses spiralled; things got worse;
the teacher felt beleaguered, cursed.
Each group was asked to write their own,
which caused a lot of them to moan.

To his surprise when he gave up
labouring on comedy stuff,
the atmosphere felt more relaxed;
Sir's confidence crisis had passed.

# Playtime

The young girl always liked to play,
there seemed to be no other way
to rejoice in life's joy each day.

She's let imagination run
wild always, having lots of fun;
drained by laughter when day is done
and the upbeat songs have been sung.

No matter now she is so frail,
old lady tells rip-roaring tales;
her wisecracks are beyond the pale,
sense of humour keeps her so young.

# Turning

No one told her turning forty
would make the woman feel naughty,
wanting to take down the haughty

by a peg or two at the least.
This milestone saw something released
as restraint and shyness decreased
and her twinkle became a gleam.

Now when she thinks she should be quiet
urges arise to start a riot,
eat sweets and cakes, give up diets,
make sure nothing is as it seems.

# Nuts

Nadine could never get enough
of cashews, Brazils, hazel nuts.
She ate them with a lot of glee
and relish, it was plain to see
her date would be on to a winner
if he served them up for dinner.

She fell for Tom, a lovely man
who proved to be her biggest fan.
The only problem that arose
was allergies - a savage blow:
when she had peanuts now and then
her boyfriend grabbed his EpiPen.

# Giving Up

Melissa loves her cigarettes,
she cannot help feeling upset
about cutting back, or worse yet

giving up. She enjoys a drink
and eating out, but would not think
twice about stopping. On the brink
of despair when she does not smoke.

Mel tried her best with chewing gum,
she bit her nails and sucked her thumb
in a battle not to succumb
until abstinence was revoked.

# Farm

Living on a farm, wondered how
to break away from sheep and cows.
There must be much more to be seen
away from her milking routines.

She left her parents, moved away,
spent time in London watching plays,
living it up, visiting stores,
but after two months she got bored

of crowds of people, dodging cars,
soon found herself avoiding bars.
Could not pay exorbitant rent,
Returned home but glad that she went
because now she can see appeal
of watching calves born in a field.

# Attire

Starting the Spring day wearing jeans,
wind softens slightly so it seems
high time for an intermission;
pale sunshine gives her permission
to switch to a skirt, sweatshirt dropped
in favour of a cotton top.
After lunch outside wearing shades,
wind and rain forces her to trade
light jacket for coat, time to change
back again to the winter range.

# Yucca

Takes his time pruning bushes, trees,
making sure they have no disease.
Loves to trim and shape his hedgerows,
relieved he has no lawn to mow.
The Yucca looks after itself,
always seems to be in good health.
But one day stops to look inside,
discovers the plant's darker side:
crowding out all the fresh and green
are daggers, rotten and obscene.
Recoiling, he cannot return,
aware the horror must be spurned.

# Flamenco

Brit thought that he would find in Spain
bullfighters and a lack of rain.
On day one he went to a show
to see the famous Flamenco.

After watching the ladies dance,
the man was glad to have the chance
to chat to his waitress awhile
in broken Spanish with a smile.

She was disappointed to see
the man had wine and not tea;
quite shocked he ordered paella,
and had not brought an umbrella.

# Slippers

Slippers have held a special place
in Lynne's heart since childhood, her face
brightens at the thought of her pet
guinea pig. Never feels upset;
Cheeky enjoyed life, had his say
right up until his dying day.
Having always slept on Lynne's shoes,
chose her slippers for final snooze.
Kept that pair, remembers her boy,
a symbol of comfort and joy.

# Silver Salver

Going on courses, staying at hotels,
the woman knows only too well
that she does not like haute cuisine:
There is not much food to be seen
beneath a silver salver dome;
eats better when cooking at home.
Minuscule portions leave her cold,
bits of fish, apparently sole.
Would much prefer to get to grips
with a large plate of cod and chips.
The only way to finish pleased
is clearing the board of its cheese.

# Repeat

Kim liked to settle down to bare
her soul about each failed affair;
In the end her friends became bored
by the tales they had to endure.
Then one day all her colleagues learned
that the tide had suddenly turned.
Life is not a trial any more
since finding someone she adores.
For now red eyes do not glisten
Kim talks a bit less and listens.
"Just dump the loser, don't think twice"
is her relationship advice.

# Blackberries

Revisiting a childhood route
the man finds changes are acute:
Traffic congestion has arrived,
few blackberry bushes survive.
Turns away from tangled brambles
to recall days when he ambled
down this lane to gather his haul
of lush berries, no way at all
could his siblings ever compete.
The lad's dominance was complete.
He hailed himself, while on a high,
co-creator of Mum's fruit pies.

# Lift

Jonny had felt pleased to be stuck
in a lift with a young au pair;
Thought it was worth trying his luck
so said she had beautiful hair.
The Spanish girl just rolled her eyes,
seemed unimpressed with his routine;
flirtation attempts seemed unwise
with someone so clearly not keen.
In this awkward situation
he felt there was tension and stress;
something got lost in translation,
emergency button was pressed.

# Beautician

During hand massage Gail can see
an opportunity to let
herself indulge in fantasy
looking at beautician Annette.

She relishes her manicure
then having long nails painted pink;
makes eye contact, then feels unsure
of her feelings or what to think.

As the woman leans over her,
Gail receives a waft of sweet scent;
a range of vivid thoughts occur,
it seems like high time that she went.

# Vicar

The vicar stands before his flock,
and spends a moment taking stock.
The church is packed - why is this so,
do folk expect a special show?

With Sunday sermon in his hand
he wracks his brain to understand.
What can have happened overnight
to make the locals see the light?

Then man remembers with a smile,
camera crews are due in a while.
Does not mind what made them appear,
just happy these people are here.

# Lukewarm

Would insist on drinks being chilled,
her water had to be distilled,
while two, but not three cubes of ice
when drinking in a pub was nice.
Refreshments served to her lukewarm
were guaranteed to cause a storm.
Then suddenly everything changed
during a summer tour through Spain;
Still thirty degrees after dark,
the woman was sweat-soaked and parched;
accepted with unbridled glee
drinks with the temperature of tea.

*Practicing Dark Arts*
*in the playground, seemed a game*
*to friends. It was not.*

*If an idea*
*is beyond comprehension,*
*embrace the intrigue.*

*Try to bury fears*
*deep within, and they will crawl*
*up to the surface.*

*View the afterlife*
*as ludicrous? Care to try*
*the alternative?*

*Will never believes*
*in karma; concept cannot*
*come back to haunt her.*

## Bundle of Joy

Jackie fiddles with strands of hair,
nibbles her nails, barely aware
they have been bitten to the quick.
Feels like her stomach has been kicked
seeing her husband's joyful face
and succumbing to his embrace.
While he is ecstatic to hear
the baby news, deep-seated fear
at the prospect leaves her stone cold
and reeling at horrors untold.

## Decorators

Janet and Steve get on so well,
but one time that the pair don't gel
is every time they decorate -
both end up in a dreadful state.

They criticise each other's work,
she moans while he becomes a jerk;
so slapdash every time he paints,
the man gets worse with her complaints.

Eventually they found a way
to get it done but have their say.
The pair stand back and watch a guy
wilt beneath their critical eye.

# Tense

Always struggling to get to grips
with Spanish, his teacher gives tips
on ways to stop running aground
in a morass of verbs and nouns.
Sam studies hard and stays up late
working on how to conjugate;
Rosa helps him relax, see sense
and take his time over each tense.

# Accident

In nightmares the accident screeched
into Paula's mind's eye each night;
the harrowing trauma reached
new levels of horror and fright.

Boyfriend driving too fast escaped
with barely a scratch on his skin;
her arm was shattered, life was shaped
by much more than use of the limb:

Lost her job in graphic design,
which was the career of her dreams.
Resolved that she would take her time
rebuilding destroyed self-esteem.

She hauled herself out of the ditch,
did exercises and fought back.
Rewarded with a finger twitch,
defence had been switched to attack.

# Types

Sean was happy to get away
from the U.K. for a few days
to catch up with his Spanish friend
in Mijas rather than Southend.

Both smiled at how the other dressed,
Cristina looked less than impressed
in her boots, scarves and heavy frock
by his tee-shirt, sandals and socks.

Played with stereotypes, poked fun
at each other in the Spring sun:
he had jamon with tostada,
she chips and a pint of lager.

# Friends

Determined to make friends in Spain
the Scottish man tries to refrain
from speaking English in the bars.
He studies the language, tries hard
to communicate without fear.
Makes progress, problems disappear;
Thanks to his positive intent
folk understand Glasgow accent.

# Quicksand

Carmen struggled for many years
with a man whose drive disappeared;
he became a lazy deadweight,
seldom worked, always turned up late.
Raul sucked the life out of her dreams,
so for the sake of self-esteem
she had to move on while she could,
hoping it would be understood
that submitting to the quicksand
was not what this Sanora planned.

# Early Night

Growing up with younger brothers,
Dad at work, beleaguered mother,
loved to escape the noise and fights
when he could with an early night.

As an adult enjoyed a rare treat
of solitude between the sheets;
told his kids he had a migraine,
felt guilty about feigning pain.

Only when his dear wife had passed
in old age was the man at last
home alone; he avoided bed
to watch a late-night film instead.

# Passed On

As a child she was full of fear
and dread at her parents' demise.
The prospect drove the girl to tears,
could not believe everyone dies.

By teenage years the terror switched
towards being forty-one day;
had grave doubts life would be enriched
when dark hair started turning grey.

At fifty she was doomed to feel
lower still, becoming depressed
about the grim hand death would deal:
non-existence and nothingness.

Only when she got to old age
was she at last able to smile;
had reached acceptance by this stage,
felt at peace walking final mile.

# Fresh Air

Jane hates it when windows are closed,
always struggles to stay composed
whenever the breeze is not there.
Needs her access to the fresh air
to keep her from feeling depressed
She has found a way to stop stress:
Her will sets a course to stay free -
Ashes will be scattered at sea.

# Battle

Assistance offered but not sought
by elderly man who has fought
hard battles throughout a long life.
Although he has outlived his wife,
a heavy stroke has felled him now.
Does not dwell on wondering how
to get by - whispers to himself,
grips walking frame; route back to health
is going to be painfully slow,
but it won't be a knockout blow.

# Made It

Laboured under an illusion
for many years, the delusion
that 'making it' was everything.
She believed that success would bring
an end to problems - stress to cease,
and all of her tensions released.

But as every goal was achieved
she felt deflated, not relieved.
While the cycle was repeated
it was just like being cheated.
Things changed when she began to care
about being here not elsewhere.

# Biscuit

Always loves a chocolate biscuit
with her tea. Dunks long and risks it
breaking into two and sinking
into a mush not worth drinking.

For a while decided to try
keeping her biscuits whole and dry,
but gave this up - just not the same
to have a drink without her game

of 'will it won't it" disappear
beneath the surface - loves the fear.
Has no plans to make the mistake
of forsaking biscuits for cake.

# Fleece

This fleece, slightly frayed, is too tight
for Penny but she puts it on
without fail for a while each night
to realise Mom has not gone.

Mom's favourite jumper was worn zipped;
to the chin even on mild days;
felt cold from toes to fingertips,
but still close and hugged tight always.

# Toaster

The toaster has been put away
in the cupboard, not used these days.
Marie still sees, staring into space
her husband's ever-grinning face.
Loved toast burnt, would give her a flash
of carbon-blackened teeth and laugh,
with crumbs clinging on to his beard.
When he died her smile disappeared.
Now in the morning usually
she can face no more than muesli.

# Nip

Jane was a lover of fine wine,
she used to drink it all the time;
rather fond of a cheeky red,
she had one or two before bed.

She did not mind switching to white
or a rose on summer nights;
on occasion had a few beers,
holding bitter and lager dear.

However, Jane would never try
a soft drink, she refused to buy
expensive water just to sip;
preferred a rum or brandy nip.

## Shutters Down

During an endless night time slows
down until it stops. Karen knows
her doubts are mutating with fear,
getting worse ... Then Dad's words appear
to her from the past, reassure
the woman that she is secure:
steel shutters slam down to keep
anxieties out, she can sleep
at last. Nightmares cannot occur
as Dad is worrying for her.


## Shower

The lad finds a room full of steam
is an ideal place to have dreams.
He prefers nothing else instead
of that water striking his head

to make him become so inspired.
In the shower he never feels tired;
amongst shampoo, sponges and soap
the lad has ideas and fresh hope.

But when the experience stops
the teenager loses the lot:
all his aspirations turn cold
and swirl away down the plughole.

# Tourist

When in a new city or town,
prefers to find her way around
on foot, glad not to use the car;
likes to chat to locals in bars.
Happy without a structured plan,
but things are now out of her hands.

Trying to help, friend Maxine makes
a range of well-meaning mistakes:
books a guided tour with no fuss,
two seats on an open-topped bus.
Car rental, she is pleased to say
is arranged from the second day.

# Photos

Ian cringes at the memories
of the Honeymoon disaster;
there are no photographs to see
of those days of joy and laughter.

He bought a camera for the trip,
which turned out to be a mistake;
the film was faulty, somehow ripped,
resulting in major heartache.

Julie took the bad news so well
back then and at can still smile these days
Memories on which the pair can dwell
are stored within in special ways.

# Chapter Three

*If you try to flee
from your problems, find they come
along for the ride.*

*In battles between
good and evil, hard to know
where the line is drawn.*

# Five Minutes

On first day at Secondary School
the English teacher seemed so cool.
He asked class to write an essay
about their summer holiday

- with a twist: all had to make sure
they covered five minutes, no more.
One girl felt so inspired to write ...
about counting chimes late one night

which came from the Grandfather Clock:
having struck thirteen it then stopped.
Moments later the girl had dared
to creep down the stairs, feeling scared.

In the hall a figure appeared
with long hair and a straggly beard.
He put his finger to his lips
as the girl's stomach did a flip.

Man opened clock door, climbed inside,
it looked like a great place to hide.
Then he was gone, girl left alone
rooted to the spot, turned to stone

... Pen comes to a halt on the page,
the story stops at a key stage.
One glance at her watch is enough:
the five minute limit is up.

## Cake

Two friends exchanged glances of doom
when Tammy's cake was presented;
the pair were handed fork and spoon,
refusal would be resented.

Melanie had a slender slice
and did her best to look willing;
Robert struggled to be enticed
to taste something unfulfilling.

When both could not take any more
the plan of escape was agreed;
Mel collapsed on the kitchen floor
while Rob hid behind the settee.

## Cool

Maxine never loses her cool,
she counts to ten, and as a rule
avoids being made to look a fool

despite all the efforts to goad.
Her head sometimes wants to explode,
but she chooses a different road
and refuses to take the hits.

When classmates try to make her down,
girl bites her lip and makes no sound,
then when no one else is around
punches pillows until they split.

## Last Minute

Barry likes to do everything
at the last minute, on a wing
and a prayer. He will often bring

his homework to school very late;
seems unable to concentrate
on work in hand, anticipate
that there might be a better way.

Relishes adrenaline rush,
the youngster always needs a push,
but never seems to worry much;
he happily lives for the day.


## Divorcees

New couple proceed carefully,
tentatively trying to see
how their lives could be together.
Divorces brought heavy weather,
while both carry bruises and knocks,
emerging from a state of shock.
Is it too soon for Christine's son
to meet John's daughter? Deed is done;
kids get on like a house on fire,
one extrovert, the other shyer.

## Sausage Roll

Stomach turns over buffet food
fingered, he is not in the mood
to tackle a sorry sandwich
or dips too long out of the fridge.
The sad selection takes his mind
back on a delicious rewind:
fun-filled, full fat flaky pastry
made by his girlfriend - so tasty!
Lost his heart to her sausage rolls.
Nasty stuff on sticks rot his soul.

## Partners in Crime

When the old friends came together,
no matter the passage of time,
they shared such fun with each other,
reverting to partners in crime.

The in-jokes came back to the fore
all teasing remarks were revived;
they laughed till they could take to more,
and both of them felt so alive.

Then suddenly his eyes met hers
and they dropped the breezy and bright;
a special moment had occurred,
but both preferred to keep it light.

## Lie In

Jill never strays too far from bed,
lie-ins are always in her head.
Takes every chance to go to sleep,
such a struggle for her to keep

conscious; if friends want to see Jill
there is a window: two until
four or half past, they need to plan
to catch her awake if they can.

## Protégée

The teacher had searched far and wide
for a protege, Sheila tried
to find someone worthy of pride.

While the woman has failed so far
she feels that there must be a star
who can play a little like her
waiting patiently in the wings.

Sheila is the best, no debate,
for now; her grand piano waits
and bides its time, anticipates
new fingers on keys, better things.

## Direct

Without fail, Michael's Spanish friend
is more direct than him, she tends
to get heard. Englishman depends

on a roundabout route with words
like 'if it's no trouble', absurd
that his message is often blurred
and leads to confusion all round.

Paula urges the man to say
what he wants, in assertive ways;
but in the moment fades to grey,
neither black nor white can be found.

## Rolls Royce service

Maureen, Estate Agent Supreme
is always on a mission, means
business - finding villas in Spain
for British expats made her name.
A perfect home for everyone
will be located in the sun
by a woman who truly adores
the job: Rolls Royce service for
each client, all keen to thank her -
the Queen of the Costa Blanca.

# Scrabble

The master of the Scrabble Board
loves word games, and can always see
the best route to triple word scores.
He knows that vocabulary

is important but secondary
to strategy - good players must
be closed down, boxed-in, not left free
to rack up high scores, go for bust.

Weak competitors are such a bore
with their poor tactics and slow play;
he wonders what he plays them for
and ruthlessly blows them away.

Frustration is mitigated
by selecting the 'Q' and 'Z';
Ninety-five leaves him elated,
another great game put to bed.

# Dryer

Janet loathes using hand dryers
in public bathrooms, uninspired
by smudges made by strange fingers,
gets out quickly, never lingers.
Faced with the dreaded toilet seat,
woman beats a hasty retreat.
She much prefers to go at home,
with her own familiar chrome.

## Theme

Loves music so much, special scenes
in life seems deserve a theme.
When enjoying a nature tour,
he much prefers classical scores.
Big cities favour jazzy riffs
rock and roll gives pub crawls a lift.
Most of the time assigns to friends,
a jaunty tune when they descend
to drink his beer. Yet with his wife
haunting ballads punctuate life.

## Jam Tarts

Box of supermarket jam tarts
takes the young man back to the start ..
Mum used to bake them each weekend,
mince pies sometimes, it would depend
on time and her inclination.
Boy could not resist temptation
to sneak in and steal quite a few.
Mother never said, but she knew
they loved her culinary touch
and she enjoyed cooking so much ..
These shop-bought confections are grim,
likely to end up in the bin.

# Rescued

On the day she was rescued, cat
hid from family in the flat.
They loved him, but keen to ensure
tabby's future would be secured.
No longer jabbed in play by kids,
feline succeeded in his bid
to escape to a better life.
Adored by the man and his wife,
dear Angel has been rebranded,
his skinny frame much expanded;
has a range of toys, beds and bowls
as well as deluxe scratching poles.
Pair won't forget lady trying
to say goodbye without crying;
heartbroken, left with even less,
facing home being repossessed.

# Race

Whatever happened to the chap,
however bad, he had the knack
of laughing it off with a grin.
So determined not to give in,
he battled through each wall of pain,
bouncing back time and time again.
To lift morale and feel nourished,
managed to end with a flourish:
Reached life's finish line with a smile,
and a bow to the crowd in style.

## Cowboys

Watching his grandson playing games
online, it does not seem the same
as the fun he enjoyed at school
when Cowboys and Indians ruled.
With his friends, at a breakneck pace
scalps were taken, gunfights took place
when chance to do battle arose.
These days sheriffs are not deposed
and folk don't flee or go to ground
when man with no name comes to town.

## Migraine

Amanda struggles with a migraine,
nauseousness with pulses of pain,
feels so wretched in the workplace.
Opens her eyes to see the face
of the cheeky guy from accounts.
He tries his best but no amount
of chat up lines or flattery
will win her over - can't he see
how sick she is feeling today,
and for once stay out of her way?
When this irrepressible wag
asks for a squeeze of her tea bag
he becomes less inclined to flirt
after she throws up on his shirt.

## Selfish

Rosie saw red, and left the room;
how could her big sister assume
it would be okay to accuse
her of being selfish? Refused
to accept behaviour like this;
would give future catch ups a miss,
withhold her opinions, advice
and try not to be quite so nice.
But then everything was okay,
Kath said 'Sorry, had a bad day.'

## Tank Top

Man wore a tank top his youth,
coloured beige - he played fast and loose
with fashion in the seventies
but forty years on feels displeased

to see himself in photographs
with lemon flares, looking so daft.
Cannot believe his bouffant hair
and floral shirt - how did he dare

to wear this in a public place
and manage to keep a straight face?
And yet the man has much to learn,
he still has the chunky sideburns.

*Told she was evil*
*as a child, the boy grew up*
*languishing in shade.*

*Misfit finds a friend,*
*but not at school; secret girl*
*only seen by him.*

*Empowered by thought*
*that classmates cannot see steel*
*behind her sunshine.*

*Sat in the cafe*
*break-up was toasted by ice*
*cubes clinking in glass.*

*A fear of the dark*
*as a child has not left her;*
*still nurtured today.*

## Uncle Mike

Dad's sedate driving paled against
Uncle Mike's breakneck speed - he meant
business as he hurtled down lanes
in every effort to maintain
his nephews' excitement levels
(Mum called him a reckless devil).
As adults, Phil and his brother
often reminded each other
of journeys which felt like thrill rides.
When learning dear Uncle had died,
they joked that the great man would grin
at a special tribute to him:
driving with one hand to the beach,
emergency stop with a screech.

## Vending Machine

A neglected vending machine
stands in the mall, now barely seen
by hoards of shoppers passing by.
It does not catch anyone's eye
as the thing no longer gets filled.
Although almost empty it still
hangs on in there - chocolate long gone,
sweets went next, all taken bar one.
That packet resisted each nudge
the machine received, would not budge.
Sole survivor caught in its coil
has a will which cannot be foiled.

## Pudding with Custard

Having lunch at the staff table
one lunchtime, Tom is not able
to connect items on his plate
with food he would appreciate
as a dirty-kneed child. Fresh fruit
and a salad could never suit
a lad who loved cake and custard;
anything chocolaty was good.
In those days it was understood
main course mattered less than the pud
Sponge would take teacher back, no doubt,
to  when his shirt used to hang out.


## Devil You Know

The couple, after fifty years
of married life's laughter and tears,
finally share the same vision:
wage no more wars of attrition,
while the blazing rows have now stopped.
They have both managed to adopt
a mantra of 'live and let live',
change yourself not others, forgive
and cherish the Devil you know.
Stay calm and happy, let things go.

## Taxi Driver

The taxi driver sighs as he cracks
a window for girls in the back;
kebab dropped then for their next trick
the drunkest is violently sick.
A cleaning fee they can't afford
is not surprisingly ignored.
Man hears assorted laughter squeals
as they stagger away in heels.
This fare came at a heavy cost
as a whole night's earnings are lost.
However, things could have been worse,
one left her mobile phone and purse.

## Baggage

Struggling with her large suitcase,
pain is etched on the woman's face
as the heavy bag knocks her shin.
She sits down and clutches her skin;
bruise will blacken, linger longer
than it did when she was younger.
However, on first break alone
will adopt a positive tone:
Wants life to have a lighter touch
having already paid too much
for years of a failing marriage
and all of her excess baggage.

## Lecturer

Robert found he could not care less
when lectures were so tedious;
he barely tried to stay awake,
did so for appearances' sake.
Would let his heavy eyelids drop
and long for everything to stop.

Now boot is on the other foot,
Rob is a teacher in a rut;
many times his presentation
is borne out vague frustration;
Bored himself, he is not amazed
when the audience appears glazed.

## Shock

The man has no chance to take stock,
he takes a step back at the shock
of his best friend's blond hair gone wild.
She was so concerned about style
and fashion, but no longer cares;
the woman he knew is not there.
Staring blankly 'Why am I here?'
has become her mantra of fear.
'There is no hope, I cannot cope!'
are the words she says on a loop.
He does not speak, but takes her hand
and prays hard that she understands.

## Romanian

Polish man shivers, tries to shake
his lingering cough, needs to make
his damp flat warmer. Double-wrapped
against the cold, his face is slapped
by the wind as he walks to class,
a three mile trek.

Arrives at last,
and in the classroom's central heating
fatigue from work starts defeating
failing efforts to stay awake.
The man is determined to take
English exams, then move away
from factory night shifts every day.

Back at home beside the gas fire
and its single bar, he aspires
to more than dining on a pear
and falling asleep in his chair.

## Civil

Officer from the Guardia Civil
approaching slowly is quick to instil
a chill in the foreigner stood nearby.
The man conjures up the courage to try
to speak, but suddenly feels shocked and stunned
and unnecessarily overcome.
Despite the policeman's forbidding frown
the tourist knows only too well, deep down,
that asking for the time is not a crime.

## Rottweiler

Jackie's Rottweiler is her life;
won't let her go under the knife,
but sees her dog is plainly gripped
by discomfort, pain in both hips.
Remedy comes not at the vet's,
but when her Princess gets all wet.
At the hydrotherapy school
her girl is transformed in the pool.
When guided gently, legs kick out
with utter joy. There is no doubt
that each time the dog is treated
dysplasia seems defeated.
Jackie loves to see Princess laugh,
this canine loves her healing bath.

## Main Man

The Main Man was a true one off,
he could be quite a scary boss;
but beneath the rough, gruff and tough
lay kindness and sensitive stuff.
So fiercely loyal to his staff,
Pete was always up for a laugh.

And when the Main Man passed away
you could not keen his team away;
they all turned up, the Church was full
for the china shop's raging bull.
His family were overcome
by love and respect in the room.

# Hand Cranked

Breaking down on the motorway
was a bad way to start the day.
Her heart sank when electrics failed,
she knew the cost this would entail.
Sat silently while car was towed,
still coming to terms with the blow.
Managed to raise a little smile
dwelling on comedy awhile.
Loves Laurel and Hardy movies,
would much prefer their model T.
A lot of heartache could be stopped
with a hand crank and open top.

# Half Full

Bill has always seen his pint glass
as half full at least; gets up fast
and hits the bar without a sound
to buy his friends another round.
Shares his sense of fun and delight,
makes sure the lads have a good night.
Does not tell them that he is sick,
staying positive does the trick.
Will not get the chance to grow old,
but won't go with stories untold.

## New Year

On the verge of a new decade
feels will to live starting to fade
and hopes for the future degrade

as she looks down into her cup.
Often feels she has had enough,
but these days just wants to give up
with no reasons left to believe.

Then movement on tea surface shows
despair ebbs and flows, comes and goes
like a ripple. Wrinkles her nose,
smiles to herself this New Year's Eve.

## Allotment

William loves the great outdoors,
and knows he will not get bored
on his allotment each weekend.
Blissfully happy, the man tends
to his plump potatoes and beans;
the earth-dusted vegetables mean
more than he can ever express.
Grandchildren know he has the best
of overflowing sweetie tins
in the shed for them to dig in.
Man relishes the joy they bring,
rejoices at fresh shoots in spring.

# Chapter 4

First time she heard them
girl flinched, but came to embrace
the voices within.

Darkness has no hold;
be delivered from evil
through eternal light.

## Cat's Eyes

A really curious shop can be found
along Scratch Pole Lane. If you look around
the female owner does not make a sound,
but remains in the corner and observes.

She slinks over if you want some cat things
a kitty brooch or some feline earrings.
Attentive and tactile, she almost clings;
the attention she gives is her preserve.

When you are browsing, beware a loose thread
visible on your jumper. Use your head -
she may just swipe, wear a tee shirt instead.
The woman has instincts which must be served.

You must not ask about a doggie toy
that is not an enquiry she enjoys;
quite different body language is employed
she sniffs and backs away, gives you a swerve.

If you enter wearing citrus perfume
owner stays on the other side of the room;
the lady will hiss, but people assume
she is either allergic or disturbed.

Don't comment on her piercing green eyes;
giving your opinion is most unwise;
narrowed to slits, you are viewed as a spy
and left feeling disconcerted, unnerved.

The shop is not seen to open or close,
she is never spotted, people suppose
that the owner lives nearby, comes and goes,
but no one knows. Enigma preserved.

# Imperial

The Spanish student is so confused
'Why are imperial units used
alongside metric in the U.K?'
Her teacher does not know what to say

about distance still measured in miles
although kilometres are in style
with young people who don't measure height
in feet and inches. They've seen the light!

While grams and kilograms can be found
many weigh themselves in stones and pounds.
Even football on TV has its shocks:
offences in the eighteen yard box!

# Poison Pals

While she's happy most of the time,
attempts are made to undermine
contentment by colleagues at work:
under their cynicism lurks
a snide remark, dig or a slight.
Some attempt to spoil for a fight
when she says that it is unwise
to constantly catastrophize
Knows peace and joy have their uses,
she won't stew in others' juices.

## Paper Hat

Each Christmas Katherine is aware
that her grandfather is still there.
Pulled special crackers with his cat,
in an ill-fitting paper hat.

The man's sense of fun knew no bounds
as he laughed and played, clowned around;
children found it hard to keep up
with grandad's overflowing cup

of joy. Kate can still hear him roar
at corny jokes, all heard before;
the dear man seemed to be at home
with plastic toys, moustache or comb.

## Advantage

Gail hitches up her shorts, biting
her lip as she keeps on fighting
to stay in the game. Swipes at air
while sweat starts dripping from her hair.
Stretches taut limbs, then lifts shoulders
which makes the woman feel bolder.
As serve is returned, grits her teeth
and digs deep to find self belief.
A surge of energy is found
to come back from love forty down.

## Heavily built

Never thinks of himself as fat,
annoyed if someone calls him that.
Insults will never be condoned;
he tells people he is big-boned,
barely needs to look at a roast,
before gaining weight more than most.
Always gives diets a wide berth,
while healthy food seems to taste worse.
Reassured no need to feel guilt,
he is just so heavily built.

## Reflection

Looking into mirror deeply,
her reflection looks completely
different now. Sadness, frowning
has replaced the larking, clowning
expressions with her big brother,
pulling faces at each other.
When he died seven years ago
the girl had nowhere else to go
for fun which really matters;
all the glass for her has shattered.

## Finance Folder

He has her finance folder still,
will keep the paperwork until
she comes back, hopefully less shrill

without the gripes, groans and moans
to discuss accounts in calm tones.
For now man is happy alone,
licking wounds with a lot to learn

about empathy, love and more.
The dear partner that he adores
has grown tired of being ignored
and she has no plans to return.

## Cross

Woman's grief has come at a cost
to her mind, but to deal with loss
Jan often thinks about the cross

that her beloved Mammy wore.
She would stand smiling at the door
of her room, then kiss it before
she knelt down to pray before sleep.

Jan sees her when she shuts her eyes,
can feel the laughter deep inside;
joy surges through the tears she cries
now Mammy's cross is hers to keep.

## Masterplan

Young mother is oblivious
to all the chaos on the bus:
loud music, shouting, every cuss

fails quite dismally to distract
or make her feel drawn to act.
All the hubbub has no impact
on the woman's life masterplan.

She smiles and is barely aware
as some girl's poke fun at her hair;
jostled by lads, she does not care
watching son asleep in his pram.

## Legroom

Always books extra legroom seat
on the plane - determined to beat
fellow passengers to retreat

through emergency exit doors.
It is a cost he can afford
in order to claim his reward
to get to be first down the slide.

The problem is he cannot swim
and crashing at sea would be grim;
this fact keeps bothering him
so keeps life jacket by his side.

Richard Seal's Strands

## Puppet Show

Rich used to put on puppet shows
just for Mike, the lad's little bro;
the two boys closed ranks, both would know

that their sister could be involved
in most things, but not this; turned cold
at request, girl had to be told
that her presence was not allowed.

Christmas was another affair -
the brothers showed Jo that they cared:
gave her a hug, clips for her hair
and three was no longer a crowd.

## Tortoise

The tortoise and the little girl
had something special going on;
Jane had fun spending time with Pearl,
the one friend she relied upon.

The reptile loved the human's lap
and snuggling on the girl's bed;
felt at home and would often nap
next to Jane on the couch instead.

While Pearl may have had a hard shell
she was tactile, soft and gentle.
Forty years on, alive and well,
still makes Jane feel sentimental.

## No Trouble

Young woman wanted you to know
she was glad to go with the flow;
so keen for friends to be aware,
Alison took greatest of care

to listen to opposing views.
The girl could never be accused
if truculence or taking sides
as she kept her mind open wide.

As an adult, kept on trying
to please everyone while dying.
The very last thought to occur:
they would get no trouble from her.

## Christmas Tree

Looking into the Christmas tree,
man feels as happy as can be,
with lots of nostalgia for free:

His little sister's frosted bell
was made when she missed school, unwell;
brother fell under festive spell
with his glitter-coated toy car.

The fairy on the top was Mum's,
still aglow after years of fun;
grown up son prefers snow to sun,
sat amid lights, baubles, and stars.

## Black Book

Discovered after decades lost
under paperwork in a box
in the loft, his little black book
was well worth a nostalgic look.
Looking at each number, address
made him smile. What happened to Tess?
Thinking of her brought back tingles,
butterflies and heart skips mingled
with sadness that they had lost touch.
He hoped she would not mind too much
if he called her up for a chat ..
but something had put paid to that:
the pages were there except one,
details of his first love had gone.

## Claire

When he bumps into Claire again
twenty years on, frisson remains;
while she flirted with all the boys,
he loved the attention, enjoyed
the way she always made him feel.
Then one day the girl let him steal
a kiss. This comes back to him now
seeing her smile; no idea how
to stop blushing. Emotions laid bare
as Claire still twiddles with her hair.

# Richard Seal's Strands

At the very end
that look the old man had had
at birth has returned.

Can never forget
his past indiscretions, she
pretends to forgive.

Colleagues get upset
by her positivity -
shaft of light in gloom.

Refused to be dragged
down by harbingers of doom;
smiles would wind them up.

Always enjoys cold;
eschews summer to snuggle
down deep in jumpers.

## U-Bend

No-one who knew Chris found it strange
that his phone was top of the range.
It never left the lad's right hand
which led his friends to understand

that they would play second fiddle
to the mobile. In the middle
of talking Chris would break away
to check out what blogs had to say.

One day addiction took its toll:
his phone fell in the toilet bowl
as he flushed; it met a sad end
somewhere way beyond the 'u bend'

## Object

When young Jimmy was alone
he found beneath a pile of stones
in the garden what was surely
a precious object; securely
he wrapped it with paper and string
then carefully buried his thing.
Felt thrilled until he discovered
that big brother had uncovered
not one small bottle in the earth,
but five large ones, and got there first.

## Smart in Suit

He always feels smart in his suit,
Business like, held in high repute.
Life seems ordered in a white shirt,
a pair of cuff links never hurt;
The man is not entirely sure why
the secret lies in a good tie.
On casual attire much less keen;
he feels so scruffy in his jeans;
hates tracksuits, it is plain to see
tee shirts and shorts are slovenly.

## Laugh At

Brittany loved to have a laugh
at workmate's expense; all the staff
fell victim to the woman's sneer,
spiteful giggles would disappear
barely hidden behind a hand.
People struggled to understand
her motives, but no one asked why
she smiled with lips but never eyes.
Then her pretend pregnancy prank
backfired badly and the smirk sank.
Colleagues said that she looked good plump
while they fondled her baby bump.

## One-to-One

When he stopped doing group classes,
Patrick, at first, missed the masses;
behavioural problems were gone
but felt flat teaching one-to-one.
He sensed a certain lack of spark
which had come from banter and larks.
However, in time he came to see
the true value of empathy;
helping students feel positive
about themselves, had much to give
when focusing on learners' needs
and how each of them could succeed.
But the man would never lose sight
of laughter and keeping things light.

## Novel

Aspiring writer wondered why
a novel would not come - he tried
so hard to move away from verse
to no avail. The man felt cursed
never to write a piece with more
than a thousand words. Got so bored
of dwelling on limitations,
he overcame the frustration
when he finally came to see
touchstones of joy in poetry:
words concise, yet vivid and bold
allow alchemy to unfold.

## Photo Shoot

Manager in a suit endures
the tedium of a site tour;
he presses the flesh, nods and smiles
when told about brickwork and tiles.
Donning a hard hat, his new boots
were purchased for this photo shoot.
At ease with budgets in his head
he is handed a spade instead.

## Frog

Frog moped around his lily pad,
as he was often wont to do;
curmudgeonly rather than sad,
he was more frustrated than blue.

Expectation weighed heavily
on the amphibian's shoulders,
but the frog would quite readily
opt to do nothing but smoulder.

He felt as if he ought to try
to find himself a nice princess,
but he wasn't really sure why -
In truth, the frog could not care less.

At the frog ball there was a twist
which came as a total surprise;
a sweet princess bestowed a kiss
but transformation passed him by.

## Gift

The woman in her dressing down
plays with tie belt as she stares down
at a Christmas card she has found

between the pages of a book
of hymns and prayers. Can barely look
at words written by hands that shook
sometimes near the end of her days.

But now the woman is transfixed,
feels like her stomach has been kicked
by this precious gift she has picked:
'from your Mammy with love always.'

## Nice Guy

Fernando was such a nice guy.
Everyone knew how hard he tried
to help others - his needs came last
as the man constantly surpassed
himself, supporting family,
colleagues and friends, but none could see
the problems he kept under wraps.
Then their tower of strength collapsed,
the pain could be seen in his face,
before he vanished without trace.

## Crushed

The rush hour underground train, packed
with commuters in close contact,
every day creaks under the strain
of bad moods, stale air and sweat stains.
During an unexplained delay,
frustration is not kept at bay;
people cramped up in painful shapes,
unable to move or escape
spot a beetle wriggling free
from a discarded cup with glee.
Avoids being crushed, finds a crack,
scuttles through without looking back.

## Limit

After having two drinks, confused
about whether she was too boozed
up to drive. Tried to calculate
her units, involved in debate
with Maxine who told her that wine
especially with food was fine.
Catherine got the woman's drift,
it was clear she wanted a lift.
Caught herself on, avoided fuss
and danger by catching the bus.

## Hale

George was a hale fellow well met;
always full of beans he seemed set
to lead a charmed life in the sun,
going out with friends, having fun.

But then a heart scare laid him low;
the poor man didn't seem to know
where to put himself any more,
which concerned all those he adored.

Found something on which to fixate:
the loss of all his excess weight.
Calorie counts now in control,
the salad diet soon took its toll.

Whilst preaching health improvement plans
he withered to a shrunken man,
but this version of him was purged
with a festive chocolate splurge.

## Stilton

Nick always delights in desserts,
he looks at the sweet trolley first:
flirts with fancies, but always seems
to settle for brownie with cream.
His wife Maxine prefers some cheese:
a ripe Stilton makes her feel pleased.
Strong but semi-soft at one stage,
creamier, more mellow with age.

# Planet

As a boy fascinated by planets -
unknowable, unreachable masses
of rock, gases and light; from Mercury
all the way to Neptune so plain to see
the thrills and mystery in moons and rings.
However, these days there is one sad thing.
A tragedy has been barely noted:
Pluto was reclassified, demoted.
The reason for being denigrated?
Its neighbourhood was not dominated.

# Social

Organiser supreme, Louise
arranges work socials, pleads
with all her colleagues to attend
and always stays right to the end.
Despite entreaties, lovely Jane
politely and sweetly refrains.
During many nights on the town
Lou's smile sometimes turns upside down;
Often tetchy and prickly cold,
she gave Jane all the life and soul.

## Mannequin

This department store has not changed
for decades; everything arranged
in the same staid way. Staff abound
but few customers can be found;
heavily-made up women spray
perfume samples, then turn away
and look bored when they are ignored.

Shocked to see the girl he adored
at school still working in Menswear.
Does she know he used to shop there,
try trousers on just to see her?
The woman frowns as it occurs
to her that this bloke has come in
just to ogle the mannequins.

## In Florence

Once English teacher had retired,
the man refocused, so inspired
by history of art. Flourished
on each trip to Florence, nourished,
living just for the Uffizi.
Blew his mind when he got to see
Botticelli, Giotto, Titian.
Loved Rafael. On a mission
until he died to get to know
the master, Michelangelo.

# Valentine

Valentine card is hard to take.
The man has made a big mistake
by expressing florid feelings;
hearts and flowers are now dealing
his prospects a terminal blow.
She had enjoyed the meals and shows,
their time together was such fun,
but now the damage has been done.
Sadly, for avoidance of doubt,
his flame will need to be put out.

# Marigolds

At garden party Jim looks in vain
for Paula to give her champagne.
She sometimes wanders off alone
and switches off the mobile phone.

Near the hedge, hiding in plain sight
the woman stands waiting for night;
amid marigolds at sunset
she feels hollowed out and upset,
sinking in the tangerine glow
to despair that no one could know.

With his face a dark shade of pink,
Jim stumbles as he spills his drink.
He has given the food a miss
to give his wife a tipsy kiss.

## Chapter Five

Full moon fills the sky,
banishes stars, trying hard to
knock spots off sunsets.

When grandfather clock
strikes twelve, knows terror will come
if awake at one.

## Star

Mum is now incredibly frail,
walks carefully and looks so pale
much of the time. Her smile survives,
and the lady's spirit revives
when engaged in some lively chat,
especially about her cat.

Daughter attempts not to feel sad
or linger on the times they had
together when she was a child;
the girl had been a little wild,
but Mum never judged, she would laugh
and say 'Josie, don't be so daft!'

Now married for twenty five years,
Josie feels youth has disappeared;
but suddenly the thought occurs
parents were the same age as her
when they first met fiancée Tim,
and were warm and friendly to him.

Now daughter wonders who is old,
it might be her, truth to be old.
Mother was fun at fifty three,
vivacious, full of energy;
Josie's batteries are running low,
Mum is still the star of the show.

## Boss

Her boss had always looked at staff
askance, would seldom smile or laugh;
simmered for too long, turned hard boiled,
he had seemed to be tightly coiled.
But everything was different when
Anna encountered John again
but this time with his kids in tow
out shopping. You would never know
that this happy man with his son
lifted shoulder high, having fun
could possibly be the same chap.
She won't forget his Disney cap.

## Room

Jeanette has always liked small rooms,
and knows she must have loved the womb.
Perhaps in many ways she regrets
the sad fact that she ever left.
As a child she hid under beds
or inside a wardrobe instead.
These private spaces just for her
were where no arguments occurred.
Now she has a one bedroom flat
which she shares with her precious cat.

# Richard Seal's Strands

## Blip

On Mum's death, daughters were distraught,
consumed by grief, while son was caught
in confused shock; busied himself
sorting through each cupboard and shelf.
In the loft, beneath a loose board
he discovered a secret hoard
of letters tied with a ribbon
beneath some old books, well hidden.

Rocked by the content, he knew well
that there was no way he could tell
his sisters about this man's words.
So what if an affair occurred?
This correspondence should be read
by nobody else now; instead
he ensured a young woman's blip
stayed private, consigned to the skip.

## Man Flu

Harry just cannot shake his cold;
the man feels wretched, tired and old.
His throat is sore, body shaking,
head is splitting, bones are aching.
Brenda has had it so much worse
and says 'I am not going to nurse
a hypochondriac like you -
this is obviously 'man flu''

# Pushkat

Alice is so thrilled to be turning eight
and happier still to see at the gate
friend Svetlana, with companion Pushkat.
The feline has no time for idle chat,
but Birthday Girl is entranced by his eyes
and learns the creature is clever and wise.
Speaks fluent Russian, shares stories and verse,
if you feel unwell, could act as your nurse.
Take care, he could be a friend or attack,
weighs you up, holding his Bronze Horseman back.

# Green Beans

Dad loved green beans with every meal.
He enthused they were the real deal.
saying they went so well with fish,
meat and potatoes, any dish.
One day Mum, an excellent cook,
replaced them with peas. One brief look
from the man before he tucked in.
After cleaning his plate Dad grinned,
rubbed his stomach and then he said
both veg were better than sliced bread.

## Brace

May taunted her sister for years,
compounding all her doubts and fears,
about the unsightly steel brace
and the sportiness of her face.
Three years on and Bernadette's teeth
are much straighter, such a relief!
Big sister's nose is out of joint,
but she has never seen the point
of making efforts to be nice.
Bernie tries but it is no dice.
Still, she takes no pleasure at all
when May breaks three teeth in a fall.

## Overboard

Felt queasy, fried breakfast shifted
and lurched as the deck lifted
then fell. As he stood at the rail
could feel his face draining to pale.
Violently sick, eyes opened wide,
he longed to drop over the side,
abandon attempts to be brave
and end it all under the waves.
Rubbed his face, blew hard, took deep breaths
he had saved himself at the death.
Feeling brighter, he had a hunch
there might be fish fingers for lunch.

## Richard Seal's Strands

## *Darkening*

Nicola stands, barely aware
of the service; a vacant stare
and a washed-out face full of lines
demonstrates her steady decline
However, she has no idea
that her daughter is wracked with fear.
Squeezing Mummy's hand she can see
the darkening, cannot break free
from fate, there is no way to save
her from joining Dad in the grave.

## *In Print*

Sally found it hard to believe
she had been published, so relieved
her poems were in print at last.
However, when some time had passed
the words appeared to be sterile,
almost cold, with a neutral style.
It now feels like she had been conned -
the stream of consciousness has gone;
Where is the thunder shot through veins?
Just pale imitations remain.

# Rebel

Rebel the dog adores his life,
so full of fun and lacking strife;
loves his owner from head to toe,
more still than she could ever know.

The German Shepherd feels such joy
every day, such a lucky boy:
thought that life could not get better
then received his crocheted sweater.

While bliss has always been the norm,
this jumper feels so snuggly warm;
barks madly while running around,
Rebel's gratitude knows no bounds.

# Necklace

Three decades ago, down this lane
the lad learned about daisy chains.
With a sunny girl he had sat
in the meadow having a chat.
Amid giggles, freckles and thoughts
of a kiss, Diana had taught
him how to link flowers and then
life was never the same again
That neckless returns to him now
he has always worn it somehow.

## Hairstyle

Girl's pigtails were her pride and joy,
the longest in her class;
they would be pulled by all the boys,
who laughed then ran off fast.

In teenage years she wore a perm
- a striking bouffant sight;
when others copied her she turned
to braids dyed pink or white.

When in her forties, suddenly
hair started falling out.
She switched to wigs, refused to see
what the fuss was about.


## Ham

For many years the man admired
his colleague's lunchbox - never tired
of seeing her enjoy pasta;
she seemed to eat salad faster,
while sometimes panini with Brie
would generate unbridled glee.
However, her glance made it clear
his sandwiches did not come near;
with cheap ham or cheese on white bread
the man's aspirations were dead.


## Cooked

## Richard Seal's Strands

The woman was always a fan
of getting herself a deep tan.
She usually travelled abroad
to bask in the sun, never bored

of spending all day on the beach.
Jade ensured that the rays could reach
body parts usually concealed;
when sunbathing all was revealed

to anyone who cared to look
at the young women being cooked.
Now middle aged, lady takes care,
uses strong sun cream, more aware

of dangers found in hot weather.
Teased that her skin looks like leather,
like her children, prefers the sight
these days of flesh so milky white.

## Lotion-Free

Decades of worshipping the sun,
without protection, having fun
on the beach and salon-tanned
has now left the middle-aged man
with skin the texture of leather.
Finds himself branded by weather
with melanoma. At last swayed
to take care, but still avoids shade.

## Boar

# Richard Seal's Strands

Sometimes heard in the dead of night,
wild boar squeals give humans a fright.
Their messages are sent in code
across the fields and silent rows
of olive trees, to summon snakes
to rouse themselves and stay awake
ready for the hunters next day.
In order to keep them at bay,
a stealth attack will be prepared
by several disgruntled brown bears.

# Peculiar

People call the girl peculiar
friends find her incredibly odd;
baffled by her sense of humour,
they react with smiles and a nod.

However, few of them can see
what is funny about a cat
who looks like a judge, or a flea
that can hold its own in a chat.

Lucinda does not really care
that her mirth at hopscotching frogs
is not shared, folk are unaware
of her secret wisecracking dog.

# Richard Seal's Strands

*Made school better than*
*it had ever been for her*
*by being a teacher.*

*Hates swimming pool, beach*
*and sunbathing; she seeks out*
*dark corners, alone.*

*Picked last for sports teams;*
*fares better behind bike sheds*
*spying on smokers.*

*She fears for bullies*
*because she knows well the fate*
*awaiting them all.*

*Can never mistake*
*seeing emptiness in eyes;*
*shares vacuum inside.*

*Flat*

## Richard Seal's Strands

He loves life stood behind the bar,
this job is his favourite by far.
Spends quiet shifts chewing the fat
with regulars, banter off pat;
at other times he runs around,
sweating freely as crowds abound.
The only downside is flat feet,
the man smiles through pain, gritting teeth.
He knows bar work is his calling
despite arches having fallen.


## *Superman*

As a child he suffered poor health,
but not held back, fancied himself
as a Superman under wraps.
An unassuming kind of chap,

lad drew strength from knowing deep down
he had no fear or need to frown;
would always wear a secret grin,
could transform himself on a whim.

While the adult is fighting fit,
Superman has slowed down a bit.
But make no mistake, he can snap
into action after a nap.

## Cage Rattled

David's emotions were a curse,
anger got progressively worse
by the day as the man's short fuse
burned down - it had almost been used.

The problem was the growing rage,
he let people rattle his cage;
then one day, and this is so strange,
it seemed that his outlook had changed:

Dave smiles and laughs a whole lot more,
calmer, not fighting civil war;
they cannot know what lies beneath:
a count to ten through gritted teeth.

## Full Fat

On long coach trip, looks at his can
of cola zero, not a fan
at all of sugar/caffeine free.
This is not how it used to be
on school trips sat beside Daisy,
who always drove the lad crazy.
Shared pop was sugary, sticky,
and then she gave him a hickey.
There will be no nostalgic thrill
eating this green salad with dill.

# Christmas Hat

If Romeo and Juliet
had only worn a Christmas hat
they might have had some festive cheer,
skipped death scenes, enjoyed a few beers.

And Henry the Eighth might have been
much nicer to each of his Queens
if he had decided to doff
his hat to them, not chop heads off.

The tragic figure of King Lear
would have seen troubles disappear
if he had worn a Christmas hat -
kingdom might have gone to his cat.

# Nominated

Teacher smiles at the young student,
usually so belligerent,
suffering from low confidence
and self-esteem, today for once
in a happy situation.
Stunned to get a nomination
from Miss for 'Learner of the Year'.
For a moment a smile appears,
she sheds a tear then turns away
to find something cheeky to say.

## Stand Corrected

The school inspector feels his heart
drop at the prospect of the start
of another day as bad guy.
He finds it hard sometimes to try

to look as if he likes his work.
Man is tired of having to lurk
in classrooms watching teachers teach;
finds warmth and respect out of reach.

Content to move mark up a grade
every time an appeal is made;
when his groups have been inspected,
quite happy to stand corrected.

## Runt

When girl found out he was the runt
of the litter, she took a punt
on scruffy-looking mongrel pup
who she could never love too much.
With Underdog for twenty years,
his demise does not lead to tears;
her friend stood for love and laughter,
and Heaven has just got dafter.

## Once Upon A Time

Every time the man reads the words
"Once upon a time", warmth occurs
as childhood comes back into view,
re-lives stories with joy anew.

Three Bears perhaps, or Goldilocks,
excited boy with special socks;
adventures in a distant land
was how this lad had his life planned.

So, reading to grandchildren now
he hopes that they will found out how
to find magic far far away
which will illuminate each day.


## Cliffs

Walking alone on Beachy Head
Sue is filled with familiar dread;
overcome by panic attacks
she finds herself venturing back
towards the edge of the sheer cliffs.
View foreshortens, body turns stiff
when she notices a white cross.
Spell is broken, momentum lost.
It is not going to end this way,
she won't be succumbing today.

## Open Door

Throughout his life the man worried
about so much, always hurried
from here to there to get things done,
with no time to have any fun.

This bundle of nerves did not know
a heart attack would lay him low;
returning to work way too soon,
he collapsed the same afternoon.

In hospital bed saw the light,
no battles left for him to fight;
relaxed, knowing what was in store,
passed pushing at an open door.

## Hazard

Escaping from driving dangers
in the U.K. - ice, freezing fog
and rain - the hazards are stranger
in rural Spain: tractors, stray dogs,
low winter sun, blindingly bright
with no light relief until night.
But mild annoyance quickly fades
when motoring in shorts and shades.

## Scary

Since childhood, movies for Mary
have always been better scary;
loves the thrill of bumps in the dark,
while comedies, dramas lack spark.

Monsters in the cupboards are great,
they leave her in a heightened state,
and spectres in the living room
cannot come to visit too soon.

One day she saw a vampire bat
pursued in earnest by the cat;
it entered her room in error
delighting student of terror.

## Tables

Lad loved the times tables at school,
outshone his classmates as a rule
With block at eight nines overcome,
he started to have lots of fun;
able to reel them off at will,
twelve elevens a special thrill.
Now a maths teacher, scares the kids
with his truly ambitious bid;
departure from comfort zone seen
in practicing thirteen thirteens.

## Won't Be Told

The girl decided early on
that she would not be put upon;
without fail she got her own way,
made sure hers was the final say.

While growing up, stuck to her guns,
had freedom and a lot of fun ...
But things are now coming unstuck
because son is trying his luck.

With heels dug in, he stands his ground
and compromise cannot he found;
Mum is aware, as blood runs cold,
chip off the old block won't be told.

## Art Lover

While looking at the works of art,
Dean feels no more than a spare part,
however does not have the heart

to tell his date Zoe the truth.
He hates galleries, sees no use
in visiting, is it uncouth
to prefer a film on TV?

Zoe gives Dean a weary glance,
would dearly love to have the chance
to go out for a drink or dance,
but would her companion agree?

## Full

With a sense of panic gripping,
and his motivation slipping,
man blinks away sweat as mates keep
on egging him on to dig deep.
The eating contest must be won,
but this no longer feels like fun.
Longs to find a way to refrain
from forcing food - no space remains.
Rallying, won't admit defeat
says he has some room for a sweet.

## Fence

The garden wall that she sat upon
as a young child has long since gone;
her grandmother had passed away
just as August skies turned to grey.
The lady had not seemed so old
to the girl, who now felt too cold
in her favourite summer dress;
Arabella was unimpressed
when the house was sold to a man
with redevelopment plans.
Decades on the green wooden door
set in the stonework is no more.
The portal to secrets intense
has been replaced by a brown fence.

# *Chapter Six*

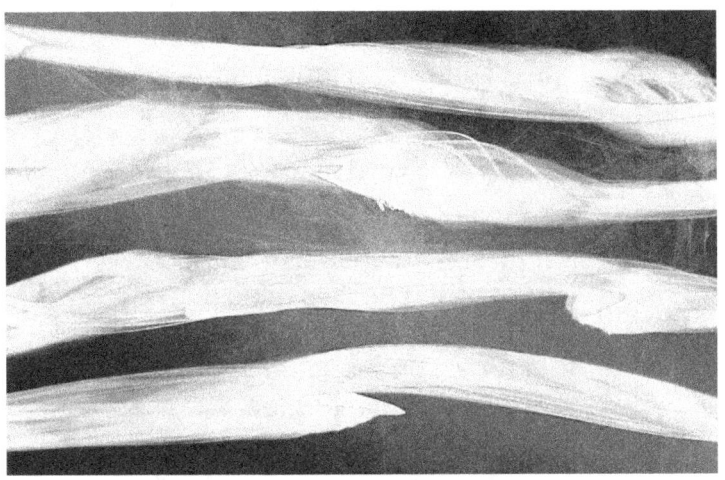

*In adversity
keep the faith, do not despair.
Love and hope prevail.*

*While life can replay
worries and fears, listen out
for laughter refrain.*

# Squashed

Having been chased around the fields
at playtime, the weary lad yields
to the girl. She gives him a kiss,
which makes the boy's thumping heart miss
a beat. Feeling confused, he sees
her break into giggles then flee.

Next day the girl resumes the chase,
but as she catches him her face
drops when he kills a ladybird
on her dress. It had not occurred
that an action meant to impress
would make his admirer feel stressed.

That night the lad has a nightmare,
and wakes with a start feeling scared.
The youngster finds himself hounded
to exhaustion and surrounded
by every insect he has squashed.
Their revenge is sweet, he is lost.

Back at school after the weekend
the lad is keen to make amends;
find his girl, spend time beside her,
show kindness towards a spider.
But moment in the sun has gone,
the blonde is chasing his friend Don.

Richard Seal's Strands

# Words

As she watched the wine being poured
woman knew she could ill afford
to let the moment pass ignored.

She watched the waiter walk away
rehearsing what she had to say;
feelings no longer kept at bay,
the lady had planned what to do.

Took dear partner's hand in her own,
with him she never felt alone;
words of love spoken in soft tones
revealed what he already knew.

# Interview

The man has no problems at all
with interviews, welcomes the call.
Embraces chance to strut his stuff,
and never finds questions too tough.

He talks about his skills at length,
has lots to say about key strengths.
It is so hard to seem the flow,
but wants to let confidence show.

The problem for this candidate
comes every time he learns his fate:
Another case of second place,
but one day he will win the race..

## *Piano Player*

As the young woman sips her wine,
feels so reassured when she finds
that the pianist seems attuned
to her mood. No longer marooned
in deep depression, shuts her eyes.
While the plaintive song makes her cry,
there is something about its tone
which shows that she is not alone.
Glass is empty, man has finished;
strength has already diminished.
He catches her eye, knows the score
and prepares to play an encore.

## *Good Man*

Rose is always stressed and manic,
exists in a state of panic
while lurching from calamity
to crisis with anxiety.
Warm and gentle, Jon stays around,
when at her worst he can be found
offering support, staying calm,
trying hard to defuse alarm.
But Rose, through her nervous laughter,
wonders what he must be after.
She cannot see Jon has no plan,
he is a true friend, a good man.

## Older

More than happy being older,
does not look over her shoulder
to linger on scenes from her youth.
Some of it was painful, in truth:
felt insecure and all at sea,
often dogged by anxiety
over exams, pressure from peers;
she longed for stress to disappear.
Since turning forty Anne has felt
content with cards she has been dealt;
more confident, knows herself well,
takes more risks now, woman can tell
she is quite likely, any day
to knock a door then run away.

## Scared

Andrew spent a whole lifetime scared
of dying, was never prepared
to discuss it. Avoided news
of natural disasters, camera crews
at the scene of murder or war.
Never at peace, could take no more.
But when the last moments came
he saw that only love remains;
on the man's liberation day
fear and pain at last fell away.

## Ovation

The man leading lengthy applause
at the end of the band's encore
doubts this is the last of their tours,
they could be tempted back once more.

Once retired they may well get bored,
miss money and adoration;
This thought strikes a discordant chord
throughout the standing ovation.

The super fan now feels aggrieved
that his band might settle for less;
hopes a comeback won't be achieved,
to be gone for good would be best.

## Crash

Cannot believe the car has crashed
he had not been driving too fast;
knows that the final bend is tight,
but he has handled it alright
in the past. The blood on the screen
is shocking, looks slightly obscene.
He cannot move or turn around,
and his wife has not made a sound.

# Finals

Her final exams had loomed large
for so long that fret was in charge;
thoughts of liberation were gone,
so beleaguered and out upon.
With Easter holiday blighted,
she hoped she would feel delighted
when finals were over in June.

But by then she had grown immune
to cutting herself any slack.
Quite impossible to relax,
while all the residual stress
was transferred into listlessness,
and she ended up feeling flat.
The only way to deal with that
would be just one more chance to cram
for another crucial exam.

# Kebab

Always worried about kebabs,
has grave doubts about the slabs
of seasoned meat - never too sure
and does not have them any more.
Likes sausages, they taste so good.
Although she wonders if she should
enquire about ingredients,
consoles herself that Gran has sense;
the lady seems to have no fear,
has eaten them for eighty years.

## Star-Spangled

Returning to New York City
twenty years on, such a pity
that Sandy is not with him now.
She was the tour guide, explained how
to keep yourself safe, see the sights
and where to go for a good night
He shyly asked if she could show
him in person where he should go.

Jim loved his American girlfriend,
still sorry things came to an end
when he went back to the U.K.
However, he wears to this day
one of her favourite bandanas
in vibrant Star-Spangled Banner.

## Creases

Standing at the ironing board
is not something the man adores;
he is quite certain, has no doubt
that all the creases will fall out
when his clothes are hung out to dry.
The only thing to make him try
to make any effort at all
is when he gets a surprise call.
Suddenly gets act together
for a red hot date with Heather

## Pin Up

The photo in the article
discussing Becky quickly pulls
his mind back to Number One Girl,
fizzing in a frothy fun whirl,
a pin up for Phil and his mates
all asking in vain for a date.

Local paper is appealing
for information revealing
any details about Rebecca,
aged forty. No one has seen her
since she left home two weeks ago,
wandered off in the heavy snow.

## Fit

For years struggled to find a place
in life, it felt as if his face
did not fit; attempted jokes flopped,
wisecracks fell flat, but never stopped
trying to be like all the rest.
Unsure what to do for the best,
threw in the towel, took a step back.
Suddenly folk seemed more relaxed
In his presence, people could see
this warm man had great empathy.
The misfit had finally found
friends were glad that he was around.

## Living the Dream

June leans heavily on her broom,
hates being a cleaner, filled with doom;
she is nursing aches once again,
and is dogged by sciatic pain.
Much too old for these double shifts,
requests for help receive short shrift.

Yet ask the woman about Spain
and a shift occurs in her brain.
She no longer looks badly frayed,
shakes off the world-weary dismay.
Clicks her fingers, does a dance,
would move there if she got a chance.

## Trip Advisor

Dear friend was her trip advisor,
been everywhere, so much wiser.
Ask any question, he would know
about pitfalls, where not to go;
at home in Paris, knew the talk
in Madrid, LA and New York.
But darkness descended on him,
checked out as the demons closed in.
News of depression was not shared,
he did not want her to go there.

# Richard Seal's Strands

Newborn chicks await
mother's return to the nest.
Black cat closes in.

Throughout her long life
she has struggled to sleep tight.
Have bedbugs bitten?

First time girl saw him
she knew that he was the one.
His heart was elsewhere.

She loved to count sheep,
but not when trying to sleep:
it might wake them up.

Adults tells the girl
schooldays are the best in life.
She dreads the future.

## Joker

Thought of himself as a joker
with quips about red hot pokers;
he bored his friends with 'knock-knocks'
but he suffered from writers' block.

The lines he used were not his own,
borrowed material caused groans;
he was often implored to stop,
but convinced he was not a flop.

Finally came up with ideas,
but they realised his worst fears.
On stage the man brought to book,
found himself dragged off with a hook.

## Gliding

Retired at last at sixty-four,
the man resolves not to get bored.
After working for forty years
now wants to try a new career.
He might enjoy deep sea diving
or try his hand at hang gliding,
so different from Accountancy.
Step by step, he will have to see.
After golf he will think it through,
just for now eighteen holes will do.

# Rain

Loves the sight and sound of the rain;
she watches it on window panes,
criss-crossing glass, making its mark
and turning the summer day dark.
Child knows the weather will turn bright
soon enough, with the welcome sight
of sunshine .. but friends come round too
and for Jacqueline that won't do.
So the girl is glad for today,
a perfect excuse not to play.

# *Workout*

With no assistants, Vincent groaned
helping a friend move flat alone.
They faced unyielding flights of stairs,
tight corners hampering the pair;
grappling with Ruth and huge settee,
manhandled her upholstery.
The scent of sweat, with grunt and groans
while pressed against walls set the tone.
Soon Vince was ready to collapse,
Ruth kept her feelings under wraps;
wiped herself down, set to go on,
but her companion's strength had gone.

# Bubble Bath

Nan took a bubble bath weekly,
relished immersing limbs creaky
and brittle in the warm water.
On last night thought of her daughter
in soapiness, silky and soft;
after several yawns, drifted off.
Slowly heat turned tepid then chill;
the lady was not found until
two days later by grandson Paul
after not answering phone calls.

# Accident and Emergency

After many long hours waiting
anxiously anticipating
what will happen in A and E
when Doctor is able to see
her injured wrist, Fran grits her teeth
and finds herself wondering why
time always crawls when surrounded by
slings and splints, little kiddies' cries.
Their parents want the end to come,
lost in pram pandemonium.
Although she thinks she is sickly,
on her turn feels guilty quickly
Doc looks shattered, ill, unsettled,
compared to him she can arm wrestle.

# Sparky

Paul dislikes his brother basking
in the warmth of their parents' praise;
it's Malcolm they keep on asking,
being the oldest sibling pays.
So what, he rewired the garage!
Paul would have done the job faster
if he had even the one in charge.
Besides, golden boy can't plaster.

The younger man would have done well
in his physics classes at school,
but had the science teacher from hell,
a man who was useless and cruel.
However, Malc was never bored,
and achievements went to his head;
brother's success would be assured
while Paul skulked behind the bike sheds.

## Chef's Recommendation

Having for once forgone madras,
to try a different dish at last,
he knows this curry won't suffice;
the man is shocked by lack of spice.
Stares at his plate, prodding the food,
sending it back would be too rude;
he knows it would be seem unkind
to give them a piece of his mind,
so eats without inspiration
the Chef's recommendation.

# Tent

Delighting in a Summer storm
the couple stayed cosy and warm
under their canvas, huddled close;
When Pete felt a little morose,
Trish cheered her up with a strip tease,
then a cheeky sleeping bag squeeze.

Man was lost to deep depression;
He tried medication, sessions
of counselling. Now body found
on a remote piece of waste ground.
Trish thinks of joy before descent,
not her Pete in a police tent.

# Passed

Beatriz felt so deeply unsure
about the multitude of flaws
that she felt she had with English.
When speaking the language she wished
not to sound so Spanish, and yet
the listening seemed even worse;
talked to teacher Mark with lips pursed
the words were just a jumbled mess.
The girl worked so hard, but felt stressed,
her scrambled mind was so upset.
The exam made her feel distraught,
forgot everything she was taught!
Bea passed, Mark said with a grin
she spoke better English than him.

## Charmer

Always wanted her name in lights,
with frame and fortune in her sights;
could not wait to feel the delight

that her celebrity would bring.
Made no attempt to dance or sing,
wanted great success on a wing
and a prayer, staying cool and calm.

Before long this approach fell flat
with reputation as a brat;
stunned by friends, ignored by her cat,
all none too impressed with her charm.

## Weather

With English weather in poor form,
a cold front was the woman's norm:
She hated fog and thunderstorms

and moaned about high winds and snow.
Autumn and Winter struck a blow
to a person who seemed to know
when the next deluge would begin.

When Spring and, at last, Summer came
it felt too hot, sun was to blame;
her misery stayed just the same,
a depression came sweeping in.

## Blood Donor

She always enjoyed giving blood,
went along whenever she could.
Two hours off work, a lie down,
cup of tea then stroll into town.
The routine continued for years,
but then overnight disappeared:
rejected, she almost fainted -
she was anaemic, blood tainted.

## Bovril

Living in Spain, the Englishman
wants for nothing; has a great life,
loves the country, is a great fan
of people, food, and lack of strife
He has no intention at all
to ever return to England;
in Granada has such a ball
but the man cannot understand
why he dreams about cottage pie,
pork scratchings, fish and chips, real ale.
He finds himself wondering why
misses Bovril most, without fail.

# Flesh

The couple tried to be discreet
by quietly slipping away;
they planned to generate some heat
on a camping trip to Pompeii.

The pair switched off their mobile phones
for some undisturbed private time;
enjoyed the chance to be alone,
relaxing with bottles of wine.

Left tent flap open for some air,
with no thought of an insect net.
Mosquitos swarmed inside to share
and savour pleasures of the flesh.

# Colours

The girl had different coloured eyes,
which caused people to be surprised,
a few of them taken aback.
Some classmates went on the attack,
calling her oddball, freak or weird;
Janette felt sad that she appeared
different. But, in time, things changed
and her eyes no longer seemed strange.
In her teenage years they became
a special feature, claim to fame.
While chilling blue turned a boy down,
she might give him a wink with brown.

## Routine

The comedian's tired routine
is more than a little obscene;
he knows that it is going down
like a lead balloon, not a sound
resembling laughter can be heard.
Retirement beckons, feels absurd
that a heckler helps the man's plight:
his comment is the night's highlight.

## Sundae

He can't see an ice cream sundae
without thinking back to that day
when she said it would be her last
before the diet - the die was cast.

By sticking to things on her list,
the girl lost weight hand over fist.
There was nothing that he could say
to stop her from wasting away.

Just when it seemed to be too late,
in an emaciated state,
she pulled herself back from the edge
He was glad she stayed on the ledge.

But eating remains a big deal,
the man dares not ask how she feels
about food - he steers clear of that
since hearing her say she looks fat.

### Richard Seal's Strands

## Sole Survivor

Meeting his school pal in the street,
Jack seizes Bill's hand, has to repeat
the account of when they were blamed
by teacher who took the wrong names.
Others had damaged a display,
then blamed the friends and got away
scot free. But the lads were okay,
headmaster was out for the day
and the affair was forgotten.
However, man now feels rotten,
as his old mate cannot recall
that momentous day at all.
Only Jack, it seems, can still see
this memory of victory.


## *Strands*

Kath focuses on her fine strands
of coloured wool; the woman plans
to make a bracelet for her friend.
She attempts to tie up loose ends
and make sense of a lifetime spent
being hurt by shards and fragments.
Relationships fractured, shattered
cause no pain now, do not matter.

<u>Percychatteybooks</u>

**Story Telling** (R)

**Somerset House**

**6070 Birmingham Business Park**

**Birmingham**

**B37 7BF**

**Registered Number 2299335**